This book is dedicated to the great-grandchildren Amelia, Braxton and Corbin.

Thank you Amelia for being the listener as I remembered the story.

The Pixie and Dixie series was created by my mother, Ella Lang in the 1950's. Ella was the best story teller making every bedtime special. This is one of the original stories told. Enjoy!

ISBN: 979-8-88722-598-2
Published: 2022
Author: Gigi (Sharon) Lang

Once upon a time there were two little mice named Pixie and Dixie that lived on Farmer Fred's farm. There were so many things to do on a farm that two little mice were busy all the time. Harvest time was the most important time of the year because it was time to prepare for the long winter months ahead.

It was a bountiful farm with lots of vegetables, fruit, farm animals like cows and pigs, hay and corn to harvest and ... a cat named Burt.

This particular day the air was crisp as early autumn started to appear.

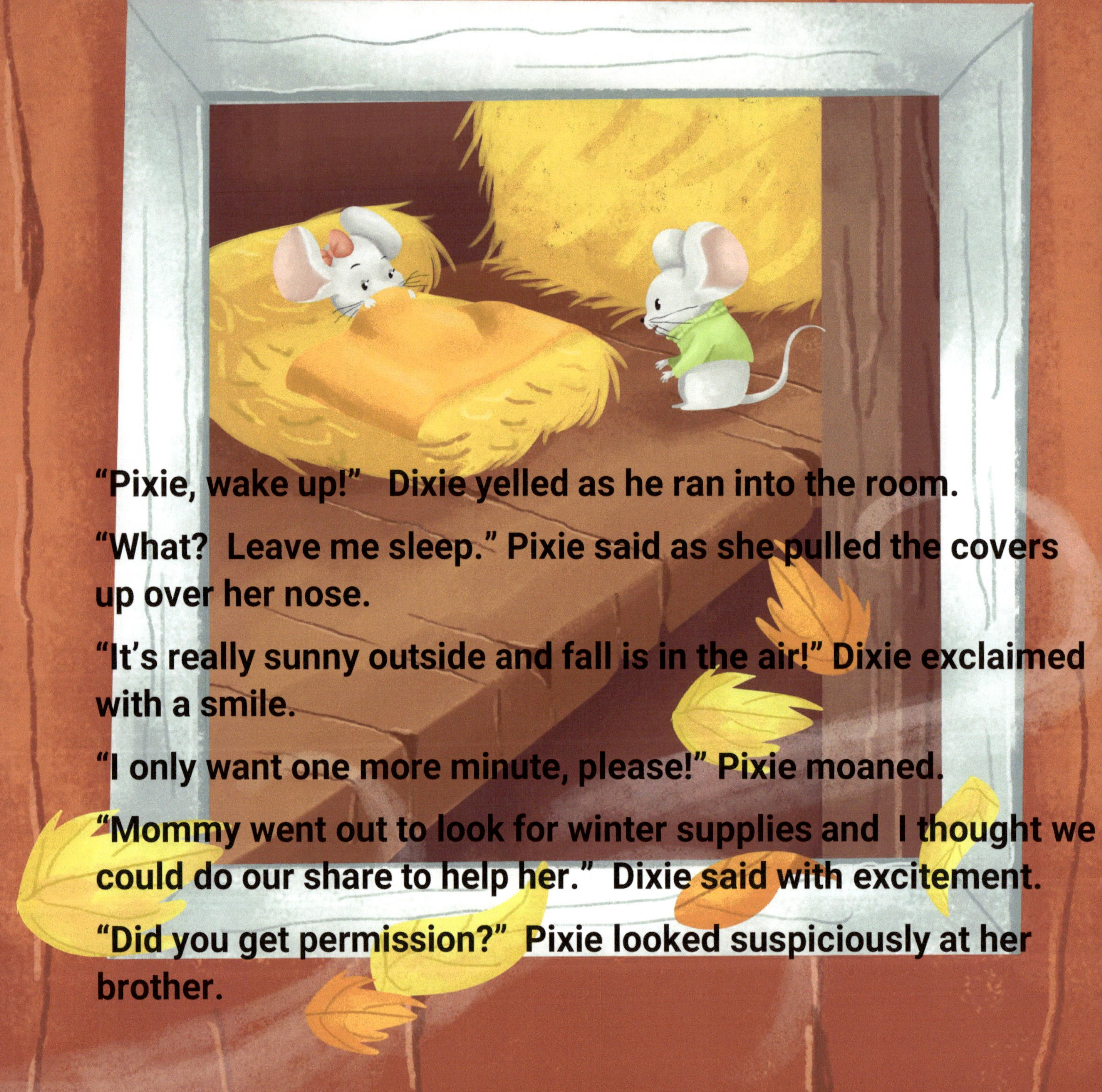

"Pixie, wake up!"   Dixie yelled as he ran into the room.

"What? Leave me sleep." Pixie said as she pulled the covers up over her nose.

"It's really sunny outside and fall is in the air!" Dixie exclaimed with a smile.

"I only want one more minute, please!" Pixie moaned.

"Mommy went out to look for winter supplies and I thought we could do our share to help her." Dixie said with excitement.

"Did you get permission?" Pixie looked suspiciously at her brother.

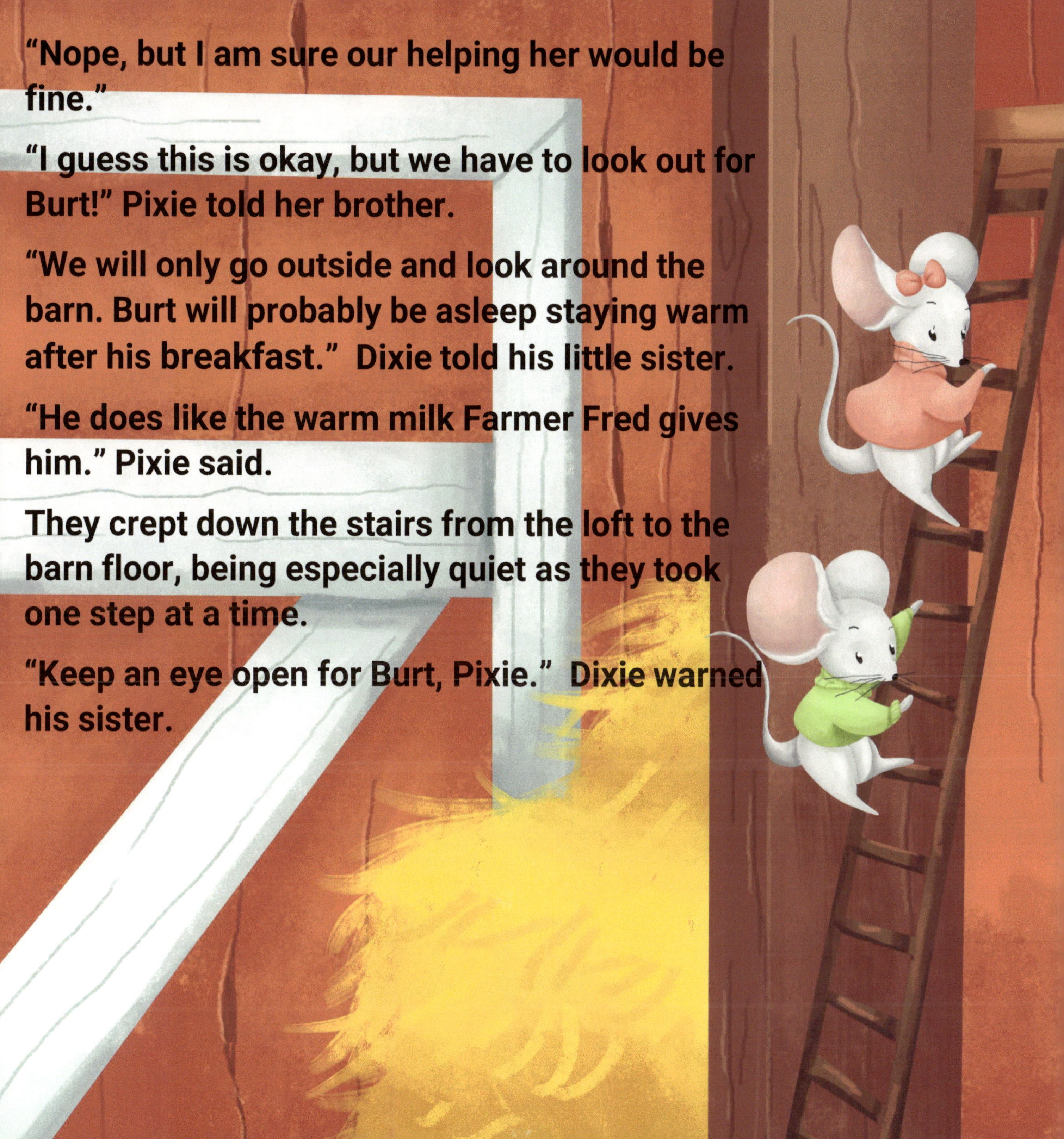

"Nope, but I am sure our helping her would be fine."

"I guess this is okay, but we have to look out for Burt!" Pixie told her brother.

"We will only go outside and look around the barn. Burt will probably be asleep staying warm after his breakfast." Dixie told his little sister.

"He does like the warm milk Farmer Fred gives him." Pixie said.

They crept down the stairs from the loft to the barn floor, being especially quiet as they took one step at a time.

"Keep an eye open for Burt, Pixie." Dixie warned his sister.

Burt was fast asleep after his morning bowl of warm milk. Just then Burt was alerted to a squeaky sound.

Burt was always listening for those pesky mice without even moving or opening an eye. After all it was his job on the farm.

Again, he heard the squeaks. He waited ever so quietly and still for the right time. He'd get those two once and for all. Burt extended his claws in anticipation and…

Just then.

"Run Pixie!" Dixie screamed as he saw Burt start to move.

"I'm so scared, Dixie." Pixie cried out.

"There's a hole over there, run. He can't go through it." Dixie told his sister.

With that both Pixie and Dixie ran to the hole. Burt was on their heels as they approached the hole.

"Don't stop!" yelled Dixie as the hole became ever so much closer.

Pixie and Dixie ran through the hole reaching the other side. Turning around they heard a thud and saw the paw of Burt sticking out with the largest claws they ever saw. Pixie and Dixie could hear the meow of Burt as he pulled his paw back into the barn.

"That was close! How do we plan to get back?" Pixie sighed.

"We will find a way, let's just enjoy our adventure." Dixie told his sister, but inside he too was worried about getting home. What would his mother say? Maybe they should have asked.

Pixie and Dixie shook off the fright from Burt and started to walk around the barn. Everything was so beautiful. The sun was shining and warm. Perfect fall day and just then…

"What are those?" Dixie said in wonder at the big ,round, orange balls.

"I don't know?" Pixie responded. "I've never seen anything like them before."

"Let's go see!" Dixie exclaimed as they ran over to them.

"They sure are big! Pixie said as she looked up at them.

"I wonder what is inside them?" Dixie said as he pointed. "How are we going to get in?"

"Do you think we can eat them?" Pixie asked Dixie.

"I'm not sure." Dixie stood there looking at the giant orange ball. "Let's climb up."

Just then Pixie and Dixie climbed slowly up the side of the pumpkin. Their tiny hands holding tight to the vine.

"Don't fall." Pixie told Dixie as the pumpkin became slippery.

"Why is it so slippery?" asked Dixie.

"There seems to be dew on everything, maybe that's the reason." Pixie said.

As they reached the top, they realized there was no way into the pumpkin. However, from that high up Dixie could see a hole on top of another one near it.

"Look over there!" Dixie shouted.

"What?" Pixie asked.

"There, a hole on top of the other one. We need to go over there to get in." Dixie said pointing to the other pumpkin.

Once inside, they were amazed at the bounty of seeds that hung everywhere. They started down the hanging chains of seeds until they safely reached the bottom. There they picked the seeds and ate as many as they could find.

"We need to gather as many as we can." Dixie told Pixie. "Winter is long."

"Yes and there's enough in here to feed the entire family all winter." Pixie said. "Maybe we should go get Mom?"

Just then they heard noise coming from the hole on top.

"Hey there!" A squeaky little voice yelled down.

"Who are you?" asked Dixie.

"My name is Chippy, and I have been harvesting these seeds for the past week for winter." he said.

"We too are harvesting seeds for the long winter for our family." Pixie said. "Maybe we can work together?"

"There are a lot of pumpkins out here, so I guess we can." Chippy replied.

“I love these seeds, have you ever had them before?” Chippy asked.

“No, I’ve never even seen them before.” Pixie said with a smile.

“Try one!” Chippy urged her.

With that both Pixie and Dixie began eating.

“Yum!” Dixie said. “Wait until our Mom eats one.

After Chippy had enough to eat and gathered some up to take home Pixie and Dixie heard more noises from above.

"Did you hear that?" Pixie asked. "Do you think Chippy is back?"

"I don't know what that is!" Dixie replied. "Maybe it's Chippy."

Outside Burt was cautiously walking up to the pumpkin he earlier saw those pesky mice go into. Burt crept low to keep from being noticed, but the rustling of the leaves and vines might have given him away. He'd get them now! They are trapped in that pumpkin.

"Gotcha!" Burt yelled down to Pixie and Dixie. "Farmer Fred doesn't like anyone taking his vegetables. He takes them to farmers market." Burt warned them.

Pixie and Dixie quickly tried to put the seeds back on the pumpkins strings.

"We're putting them back!" Dixie yelled up.

"Too late you pesky mice." Burt snared back. "Farmer Fred will give me a big bowl of milk as a reward!"

"Dixie, what are we going to do?" Pixie wondered.

"We can try to escape once he's gone." Dixie told Pixie.
"That could be a long time and it's getting dark." Pixie said.

"I'll go first and see if he's still out there."

Dixie carefully climbed out the hole but didn't see Burt hiding behind the large pumpkin.

"Pixie, I think he's gone." Dixie yelled down.

Just then Burt let out a loud scream as Chippy took a bite out of Burt's tail. Chippy watched earlier Burt creeping around the patch. After he took home his seeds he returned to help his friends.

"Your not getting my new friends." Chippy yelled "Run Pixie. Run Dixie, I've got him."

With that Pixie and Dixie climbed down the vine holding their seeds.

"Thank you Chippy!" Pixie yelled as they ran to the barn.

"That was close!" Pixie said. "I wonder if Chippy got away?"

Just then Dixie peeked around the corner of the barn.

"Run Pixie, it's Burt!" Dixie screamed as they took off running.

"In here Pixie. Quick!" Dixie yelle
"He's going to get us!" Pixie said.
"No, he can't fit in the hole." Dixie motioned.

"Where did all these seeds come from?" Their mom asked.

"Well, we went out to the pumpkin patch." Dixie told his mom and very nervous telling her.

"That was very dangerous, but I'm proud of the work you did today and these seeds will keep us fed all winter. Next time, let me know where you are going so we can do it together." Their mom told them.

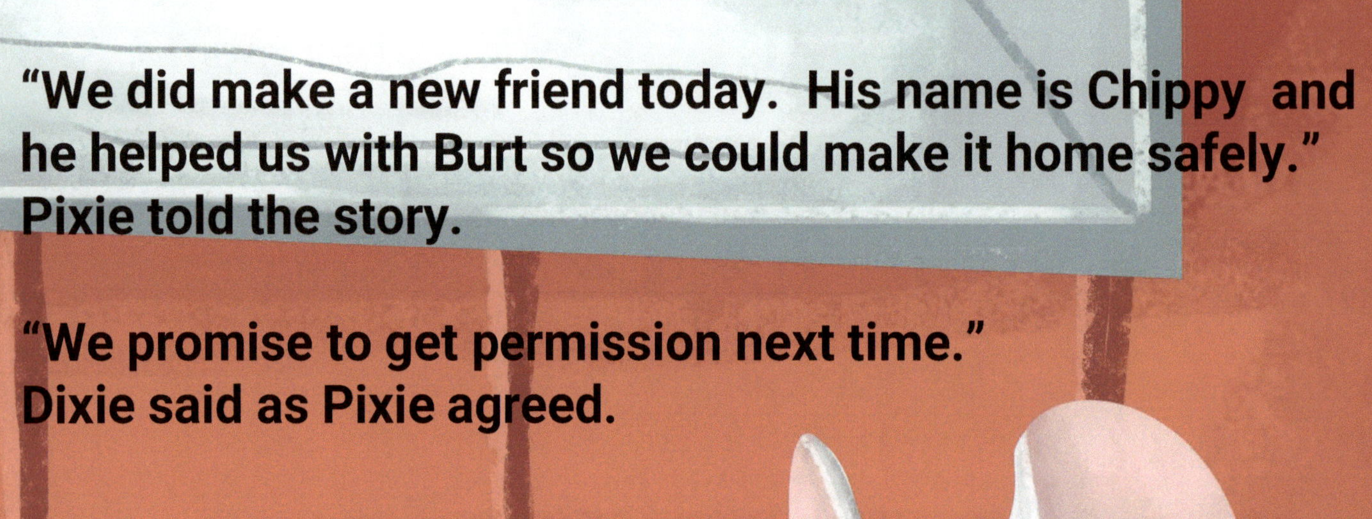

"We did make a new friend today. His name is Chippy and
he helped us with Burt so we could make it home safely."
Pixie told the story.

"We promise to get permission next time."
Dixie said as Pixie agreed.

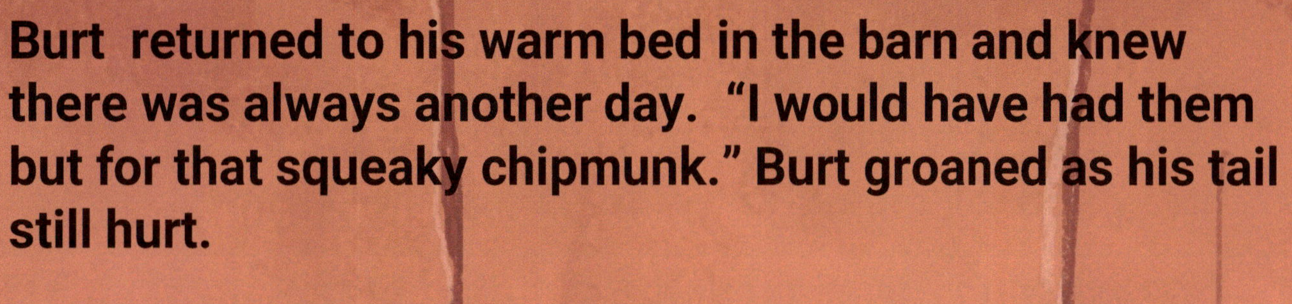

Burt returned to his warm bed in the barn and knew there was always another day. "I would have had them but for that squeaky chipmunk." Burt groaned as his tail still hurt.

He'll keep a closer eye out for those pesky mice and their little friend too... and he dreamt of his next chase.

All the mice and chipmunk families were amazed at the tale. The very next day they all went to the garden and brought back enough food for the entire winter.

As Pixie and Dixie laid in the soft bed of hay they realized their hard work helped benefit everyone but next time they will get permission.

The End or Should We Say The Beginning of More Adventures !

<u>**Fun Facts**</u>

A pumpkin, from a botanist's perspective, is a fruit because it's a product of the seed-bearing structure of flowering plants. Vegetables, on the other hand, are the edible portion of plants such as leaves, stems, roots, bulbs, flowers, and tubers.

In the 19th century, when a lot of Irish immigrated to the United States, they brought the Halloween tradition of using vegetables to scare the spirits away. In America, the Irish discovered a new vegetable, the pumpkin, which is harvested in the fall, and began using it to scare the evil spirits.

The colonists and indigenous people ate pumpkins and squash frequently in the 1600s, so gourds were probably served at the first Thanksgiving.

Pumpkins have become symbols of prosperity, growth and abundance.